BUG BLONSKY

and His Very Long List of Don'ts

E. S. REDMOND

CANDLEWICK PRESS

First edition 2018

Library of Congress Catalog Card Number pending
ISBN 978-0-7636-8935-3

17 18 19 20 21 22 TLF 10 9 8 7 6 5 4 3 2 1

Printed in Dongguan, Guangdong, China

This book was typeset in Chaparral and Bokka.
The illustrations were done in pen and ink and watercolor.

Candlewick Press
99 Dover Street
Somerville, Massachusetts 02144

visit us at www.candlewick.com

For Bug, Rabbit & Piggy

My name is Benjamin,
but everyone calls me Bug.

My mom says it's because I am super wiggly and never sit still.

BUGS THAT ARE SUPER WIGGLY

 spider

 beetle

grasshopper

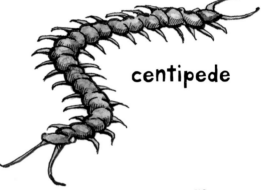 centipede

earthworm

me

But my big sister, Winnie, says it's because I am super annoying.

BUGS THAT ARE SUPER ANNOYING

ant

wasp

fly

mosquito

gnat

me!

She says that if I were a superhero with a superpower, I would be Bug-Boy with the Power to Annoy, which she thinks will make me mad, but I think sounds kind of awesome.

Wings for flying and making irritating buzzing noises

Super strength for lifting 300 times my own weight and for protection (from Winnie)

Hairy legs for sensing danger (Winnie) and for looking manly

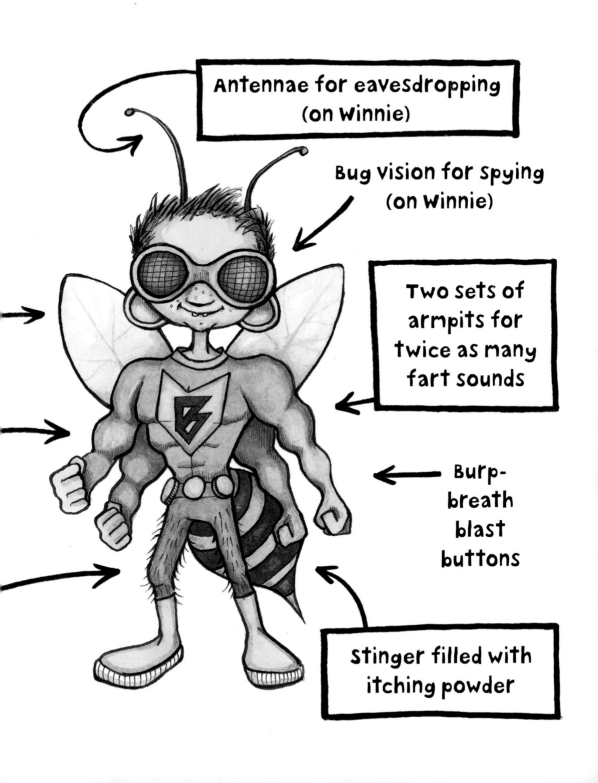

My dad says I'm impulsive and distractible.

I am not sure what that means, but I spend a
lot of time in the quiet chair thinking about
my choices.

I am writing a list of Don'ts to help me remember what *not* to do, but it's taking me a really long time to finish because I keep looking out the window and wondering what my best friend, Louie, is up to.

#1

DON'T spray whipped cream into your mouth for breakfast.

Because if you do, Winnie will yell, "MOM! Bug is spraying whipped cream into his mouth again!" and then she'll roll her eyes and call you a pig, which she thinks will make you mad, but you take as a compliment because *everyone* knows that pigs are one of the top ten smartest animals on the planet.

Then Mom will say that whipped cream is no breakfast for a seven-year-old and she'll fix you a bowl of boring wheat squares instead, which taste exactly like cardboard. Actually, worse, they taste exactly like cardboard soaked in milk, and you'll wonder if pigs eat slop for breakfast instead of boring wheat squares because they are so smart.

YUM!

WHEAT SQUARES

#2
DON'T eat boring wheat squares while hopping on one leg.

Because if you do, you will knock over your cereal bowl and spill milk all over the table and ruin Winnie's homework and soak your socks. Then Winnie will yell, "MOM! Bug ruined my homework and made a mess at the table again!" and Mom will sigh and say, "How many times have I told you to sit in your chair while you eat breakfast?"

GREAT PLACES TO EAT BREAKFAST
BESIDES MY CHAIR

#3
DON'T play Stackblox
(the most epic video game of all time)
before school.

Because if you do, you'll forget all about getting ready because you'll get the awesome idea to build the world's very first pig roller coaster, and the next thing you know Mom will yell, "Bug! The bus is here! You're going to be late for school again!"

Then you'll rush around to find your back-pack and sneakers and won't have time to change out of your milk-soaked socks.

#4
DON'T be late for the bus.

Because if you are, the only seat left will be right up front next to that know-it-all Abner Vanderpelt, whose hair is always parted and combed like he is going to a fancy party instead of school. Your socks will squish when you take your seat next to him, and he will point out that you are late, as usual, and ask you too loudly why there's a wheat square stuck to your chin.

#5
DON'T sit next to Louie during morning meeting.

Because if you do, you'll want to tell him about your awesome idea to build the world's very first pig roller coaster in Stackblox and Ms. Munster, your teacher, will say, "Benjamin, this is morning meeting. You need to be quiet now and listen," and she'll make you get up from sitting next to Louie and seat you right up front next to Peggy Pinkerton, who never stops smiling at you.

#6
DON'T climb the bookcase to get a book from the top shelf.

Because if you do,
Abner Vanderpelt will
yell, "Ms. Munster, Bug
is setting a bad example!"
and Ms. Munster will say,
"For heaven's sake, Benjamin,
get down from there! You're a
boy, not a bug!" Then she'll pair
you up with Abner for reading
buddies and you'll have to
read the book he's already chosen about the
solar system, which you read yesterday.

#7
DON'T be Abner Vanderpelt's reading buddy.

Because if you are, Abner will tell you with that know-it-all look on his face that out of all the planets, Uranus is the biggest and you'll be so happy that he's wrong for once that you'll say, "No, it *isn't*. Jupiter is." Then he'll smirk and say, "If you don't believe me, ask Ms. Munster."

#8
DON'T ask Ms. Munster, "is Uranus the biggest?"

Because if you do, it will come out sounding all wrong and Ms. Munster will scrunch her eyebrows and say, "Benjamin, that is *entirely* inappropriate," and when the whole class gasps, Abner will sit there looking all innocent and smug and pretend to be shocked by your rudeness.

#9
DON'T trade snacks with Kirby Dinklage.

Because if you do, you'll wind up with a flax-seed muffin, which doesn't taste *anything* like cotton candy like Kirby said it would. It tastes more like boring wheat squares. And then you'll have to watch him eat the chocolate-chip cookie your mom baked because there are no take-backs.

And Peggy Pinkerton will smile at you with orange teeth and offer to share her bag of spicy corn chips, but when you reach inside, there'll only be crumbs left.

#10
DON'T draw pictures of pig roller coasters during math time.

Because Ms. Munster will say, "Benjamin, this is time for math, not art," and that "drawing a pig riding a roller coaster is not a very good use of your time," and even though you totally disagree, you will crumple up your paper and shove it in your backpack.

#11
DON'T tell Kirby to QUIT it
when he calls Peggy "STINKERton"
at recess.

Because if you do, Peggy will turn to you with a weird, dreamy look on her face and you'll know that she got the wrong idea. And instead of just smiling at you like usual, she'll sigh and say, "Prince Charming!"

Then, before you know it, she'll squeeze your arms way too hard with her pudgy pink fingers and lean in with her spicy corn-chip breath and try to kiss you!

You will feel like stomping really hard on her foot.

#12
DON'T stomp really hard on Peggy Pinkerton's foot.

Because if you do, her bottom lip will quiver and she will start to cry and wail, "A *real* prince would never do that!" and Mrs. Killjoy, the recess monitor, will march over with her hands on her hips and a look on her face that means business and she will say, "Mr. Blonsky, come with me." And you will find yourself sitting in Principal Sternsly's office.

oops!

#13
DON'T ask Principal Sternsly if she was pretty when she was young.

Because if you do, she won't think you're being charming or conversational. She will wrinkle her nose like she smells something bad and blink at you for a long time without saying a word and you'll wonder if this is what Mom meant when she tried to explain that sometimes thoughts should stay inside your head.

#14
DON'T eat leftover meat loaf for lunch.

Because if you do, Kirby Dinklage will yuck your yum by saying, "That's gross," and telling the table that you are eating smelly garbage for lunch. Then everybody (including Louie) will yell, "Eeeeeeewww!" and make barfing sounds, and your cheeks will feel hot and even though you're starving because you didn't really eat breakfast or snack . . .

you'll want to dump your entire lunch on Kirby's head.

#15
DON'T dump your lunch on Kirby Dinklage's head.

Because if you do, Mrs. Killjoy, the lunch monitor, will march over with her hands on her hips and a look on her face that means business and she will say, "Mr. Blonsky, come with me." And you will find yourself talking to Principal Sternsly . . . again.

#16
DON'T make armpit fart sounds when Ms. Munster bends over.

Because if you do, it will sound like she cut the cheese in front of the whole class, and Louie will crack up like it's the best most funniest thing ever and everyone else will be laughing hard too, *except* for Ms. Munster, who will demand an explanation.

But before you can get your hand out of your armpit, Abner Vanderpelt will be pointing at you with that dumb look on his face.

#17

DON'T wear Timmy Tow Truck underpants to school in second grade.

Because if you do, when you bend over to take off your soggy socks because everyone keeps asking what that awful smell is, Kirby Dinklage will point and laugh and say that Timmy Tow Truck underpants are for baby first-graders. You will want to tell him that he still has some leftover meat loaf in his hair . . . but you won't.

TOP TEN AWFUL SMELLS

10 My sour-milk socks

9 cat food

ME-YUCK!

8 Fish taco Tuesdays

7 Winnie's girly perfume

moody

FOR TWEENS

6 My sneakers

#18
DON'T put milk-soaked socks in your backpack.

Because if you do, when Abner Vanderpelt raises his hand at the end of the day to remind Ms. Munster that she hasn't collected the homework yet, your homework will be sopping wet and ruined by your milk-soaked socks and you'll have to hand in a crumpled drawing of a pig riding a roller coaster instead.

#19
DON'T tell Dylan Farkler that Winnie wrote his name with hearts all around it in her diary.

Because if you do, Dylan will look like someone just punched him hard in the stomach and his best friend, Billy Butcher, will laugh and make kissy-face sounds the whole way home.

And Winnie will wonder later why Dylan has
suddenly stopped talking to her.

#20
DON'T tell Winnie why Dylan Farkler has suddenly stopped talking to her.

Because if you do, Winnie will look like someone just punched her hard in the stomach and burst into tears and scream, "I HATE YOU, BUG! You're SO annoying! I'm NEVER EVER speaking to you again. I *mean* it this time!" and Mom will come into the kitchen and ask what on earth is going on.

#21
DON'T tell Mom what's going on.

Because if you do, she will fold her arms across her chest and frown like she did the last time you read Winnie's diary, and she won't care that it was lying wide open on her bed in plain sight.

She will also say that Principal Sternsly called TWICE today and because of your behavior, you can't play at Louie's after school like you were supposed to, which stinks because you were going to build pig roller coasters. Instead, you'll end up sitting in the quiet chair, thinking about your choices . . .

and writing a VERY long list of Don'ts.